'Free! he shouted happily. .... America!
Goodbye to your rubbish and your poisons. If anyone asks, don't
tell them where we are.'

Allie Fox is a clever, independent man. There's almost nothing he can't make or mend. When he gives an opinion, he is *right*.

So when he tells his wife and children that they're leaving their home to start a new life, they don't argue. But Allie's 'new life' is in the jungles of Honduras. There, he says, they'll build a better world, away from money, television and all the troubles of America.

But can their lives in the jungle really be better? Can Allie stay in control the way he thinks he can? These are the questions that his family begin to ask, as the problems of the 'natural' life meet the dreams in Allie's mind . . .

Paul Theroux began writing in the 1960s but did not become famous until the 1970s. Since then, his best-selling stories and travel writing have made him a millionaire.

He was born in Massachusetts in the USA in 1941 but has spent much of his life in other countries. He was a teacher in Africa and Singapore and lived in England for many years. Many of his stories are about life in countries he has visited. His travel books are often about long railway journeys.

The Mosquito Coast was a very successful film in 1986, with Harrison Ford as Allie Fox and River Phoenix as his son, Charlie.

Paul Theroux now lives part of the time in Massachusetts and part of the time in Honolulu, Hawaii.

For a complete list of the titles available in the Penguin Readers series please write to the following address for a catalogue: Penguin ELT Marketing Department, Penguin Books Ltd, 27 Wrights Lane, London W8 5TZ.

The Mosquito Coast

PAUL THEROUX

Level 4

Retold by Robin Waterfield
Series Editor: Derek Strange

PENGUIN BOOKS

PENGUIN BOOKS

Published by the Penguin Group
Penguin Books Ltd, 27 Wrights Lane, London W8 5TZ, England
Penguin Books USA Inc., 375 Hudson Street, New York, New York 10014, USA
Penguin Books Australia Ltd, Ringwood, Victoria, Australia
Penguin Books Canada Ltd, 10 Alcorn Avenue, Toronto, Ontario, Canada M4V 3B2
Penguin Books (NZ) Ltd, 182–190 Wairau Road, Auckland 10, New Zealand

Penguin Books Ltd, Registered Offices: Harmondsworth, Middlesex, England

The Mosquito Coast © Paul Theroux, 1981
First published by Hamish Hamilton Ltd 1981
Published in Penguin Books 1982
This adaptation published by Penguin Books 1995
7 9 10 8

Copyright © Robin Waterfield 1995
Illustrations copyright © Bob Harvey (Pennant Illustration Agency) 1995
All rights reserved

The moral right of the adapter and of the illustrator has been asserted

Illustrations by Bob Harvey (Pennant Illustration Agency)

Printed in England by Clays Ltd, St Ives plc
Set in 11/14 pt Lasercomp Bembo by
Datix International Limited, Bungay, Suffolk

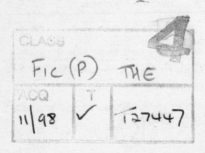

To the teacher:

In addition to all the language forms of Levels One to Three, which are used again at this level of the series, the main verb forms and tenses used at Level Four are:

- present perfect continuous verbs, past perfect verbs, *was/were going to*, passive verbs (simple aspects only and with available modal verbs), conditional clauses (using the 'second' or 'improbable' or 'hypothetical future' conditional) and further phrasal verbs
- modal verbs: *should* and *ought to* (to give advice or expressing desirability), *used to* (to describe past habits, states and routines), *must* and *can't* (to express (deduced) likelihood), *may* and *might* (to express possibility or uncertainty), *could* (to express hypothetical ability), *would* (to express willingness) and *had better* (to give advice).

Specific attention is paid to vocabulary development in the Vocabulary Work exercises at the end of the book. These exercises are aimed at training students to enlarge their vocabulary systematically through intelligent reading and effective use of a dictionary.

To the student:

Dictionary Words:

- As you read this book, you will find that some words are in darker black ink than the others on the page. Look them up in your dictionary, if you do not already know them, or try to guess the meaning of the words first, and then look them up later, to check.

My father shouted at fat people on the streets.

CHAPTER ONE

We drove past Tiny Polski's house on the way to the road. My father pointed with his finger − the one whose end he had lost while he was making one of his **inventions** − at the workers in the fields.

'Here come the **savages**,' he said. 'I don't know why they come here. Here there is only Coca-Cola, TV poisoning their minds, factories poisoning the air and the rivers; but where they come from, there's nothing. It's beautiful.'

He was talking more and more like this these days.

'I know why Polski uses them,' he went on. 'They're cheap. They don't know any better. Then he can make more money selling his vegetables.'

My father worked for Mr Polski. He mended the farm's machines, and anything which had gone wrong. He could make or mend anything. But he was really an inventor − the great Allie Fox.

That day we drove from Hatfield into Northampton. My father shouted at fat people on the streets to eat healthier food; he argued with the shopkeepers. He always thought he knew better than everyone. I was thirteen years old, and I didn't doubt that he *was* right. But I was embarrassed by the stares people gave us − a man and a boy whose clothes and voices showed that they didn't belong in town.

'Why isn't your boy in school?' someone asked.

'You don't learn anything in school,' my father shouted back. 'School is for fools. Charlie's learning what he needs to know by being with me, and by watching.'

But part of me wanted to be in school, wanted to be like the others. When I saw other children, I couldn't meet their eyes.

Father bought what he wanted and we drove back home. In the van, he continued talking without stopping. Once he said, 'You can make ice out of fire, Charlie, did you know that?' At another time, he said, 'They're all after me. They want to get me. I'm the last man in the world.'

♦

Father had been in hospital once. They took him there because he refused to eat. But that was before we moved to Massachusetts. Father was happier here, and that meant we were all happier – Mother, me, my younger brother Jerry, and the twins. I was thirteen, Jerry was ten, and April and Clover were five. Back in Maine, Father had tried to be a farmer, but it had not gone well. Here he could pretend that he was independent, and that he only worked for Polski when he wanted to. We grew nearly all our own food. Our clothes and shoes were mended, and then mended again. We had no TV and nothing to play with. We fought the sea-birds – my father screaming '**Scavengers**!' at them – for other people's rubbish and took it home to use. I was old enough to help Father around Polski's farm and with some of his inventions; the others helped Mother around the house.

'Polski owns people,' Father said, 'but he doesn't own me.'

The things Father bought in Northampton that day helped him to finish his latest invention. It was a wooden box, filled with **pipes**. Father called it Little Boy. He took it over to Polski and showed him how it worked. He lit a small fire at the bottom and put a glass of water inside the box.

'Now, wait,' he said. 'You'll see what Little Boy can do. And remember: this is just a model. Try to imagine Fat Boy.'

'I don't want to wait,' Polski said. 'I have problems. Why might I want to cook a glass of water? This year, I have too many vegetables to keep, but they're ripe and I have to pick them.'

'Don't keep them, then,' Father said. 'Sell them.'

'I can't sell them now. Prices are too low.'

'That's just typical of America these days,' my father said. 'Dentists put money into factories that make sweets. You could sell your vegetables now, but you prefer to wait. Then people will have to pay more for them in the shops – but you will make more money. It's wrong.'

'It's business,' Polski replied.

'I don't want any part of it,' Father said.

Smoke came out of a hole in the top of the box. The smell was terrible.

'No electricity needed, no moving parts. This machine will keep going for ever,' my father said proudly.

'If the smell doesn't kill you first,' Polski said.

'I can get rid of the smell. This is just a model. I think it's ready. Why don't you take the glass out of the box, Mr Polski?'

Polski carefully took out the glass. The water had turned into ice.

'Very clever, Mr Fox,' Polski said. 'But if I want ice, I go to my refrigerator.'

'What about the future,' Father asked, 'when it's no longer possible to make electricity?'

'I won't be here in the future.'

'That's typical too. That's criminal. That's stupid.'

As we drove back home, with Little Boy in the open back of the van, I said, 'He didn't like it very much.'

'No,' said my father, 'but I don't care any more.' He breathed deeply. 'America. It breaks my heart. It used to be possible for a man like me to live here.'

Back home, he was busy for some time on the phone.

CHAPTER TWO

The next day, we went shopping again. We usually went only once a month, and this was the second time in two weeks. Jerry, the twins and I all stood in the back of the van, imagining ice-creams and bikes we secretly knew Father wouldn't let us have. To our surprise, we drove past Hatfield and even past Northampton. We stopped at Springfield. We had never shopped there before, and people on the streets seemed to know this. They stared at us in the back of the van.

Father got out of the front. He was saying, 'Hats! They must have hats. It's hot there.'

We walked from shop to shop. Sometimes we bought something – hats for us children, medicines, water bottles, mosquito **nets**, things like that. More often, Father argued with the shopkeepers about the bad quality of the things they tried to sell him, and complained about the prices. 'I'm not going to pay these prices any more,' he said.

Outside the shops, Mother said to him, 'You never give in, do you?' Or sometimes she asked him to calm himself.

'This country is finished, Mother, can't you see? Finished. There's a whole world out there.' He pointed with his ugly half-finger, surprising people on the street with his loud voice.

Finally, Father bought several sacks of vegetable seeds, and we went home. Late that night, I heard Polski and Father shouting at each other downstairs. I heard Polski calling my father a dangerous man.

The next day, Father told us to get into the van. Clover asked, 'Dad, are we going somewhere?'

'We certainly are.'

to travel light – podróżować
bez dużego bagażu.

'Why haven't we packed our bags?'

'Because we're travelling light. We're leaving everything and getting out.'

I was standing next to Ma, listening to this. I said, 'Ma, what's he talking about? Where are we going?'

'He'll tell us when he's ready.' She didn't know! And we just left – with bills unpaid, dirty plates on the table and clothes in the cupboards.

CHAPTER THREE

The ship was enormous. We arrived in Baltimore in the night and drove to the docks. In the darkness, the ship seemed to go up and up into the sky. Our few things were taken on to the ship. Father gave our old van to a black man who was passing.

'Free!' he shouted happily. 'Free at last! Goodbye America! Goodbye to your rubbish and your poisons. If anyone asks, don't tell them where we are.'

We sailed in the middle of the night. We were asleep, but *ruch* *muv'ment* the movement of the ship woke me up. In the morning, we were in the open sea.

The ship was called the *Unicorn*. It was carrying machines, clothes and food, but there were two other families as well – the Bummicks and the Spellgoods. We were introduced to them at breakfast.

'You're Mr Fox,' one of the men said to Father on our first day at sea. 'You've already forgotten my name, but I remember yours.'

'Of course you do,' Father said. 'I'm much easier to remember than you are.'

That man was Gurney Spellgood. He was a **missionary**.

We didn't see much of the Bummicks, but for the rest of the journey, my father found ways to annoy Mr Spellgood. He refused to be silent before each meal, he argued about God with him. 'If God made the world,' he said, 'why is it made so badly? Why do inventors like me have to make things better than they already are?'

Spellgood had a large family. One of his daughters, Emily, was about my age, and she tried to make friends with me. She used to talk to me while I was fishing off the back of the ship. Once I complained that the hot weather had made the fish go too deep for me to catch them.

'If you think this is hot, wait until you get to Honduras,' Emily said.

It was the first time I had heard where we were going. I looked at the map of Honduras on the wall outside the radio room. Pins showed how far we had come from Baltimore, on the way to La Ceiba.

Emily never left me alone. She talked about their home in Honduras, in a place called Guampu. She talked about their motor boat on the river there, and about how nearly all the Indians spoke some English now. The worst time was when she asked what my favourite football team was. I didn't reply.

'I suppose you don't even have a team where you come from,' she said.

'Yes, I do. They're on television,' I said.

'What's your favourite TV programme?'

I couldn't answer. We didn't have a television. Father hated them, together with radios and newspapers and films. I said, 'Television programmes are poison.' That was what Father always said.

'You must be sick,' Emily said. She went on and on about her school. I didn't know what to say: I didn't have a school,

6

or schoolfriends and teachers. I didn't like Emily – she was different from anyone I had ever known. But she knew things I didn't know, and I thought that Father had lied to me. I didn't know everything I should know.

Once, when we were close to Honduras, the captain invited me up to see the ship's instruments. He didn't like my father either, but Father had mended one of the ship's **pumps**, so he had to agree that my father was as clever as he said. 'He had better be,' the captain said. 'You know where he's taking you?'

'Yes, sir.'

'You're going to the Mosquito **jungle**. Some people there have never seen a white man and don't know what a wheel is. Ask Mr Spellgood. If they want to eat, they just climb a tree and take some fruit. Most of them don't wear any clothes. It's a free and easy life.'

'That's why we're going,' I said.

'But it's no place for you,' the captain said. 'Imagine a zoo – except that the animals are outside, and the white men are inside, in their houses and churches. You look out and you see all the animals staring in at you. They're free, but you're not.'

'My father will know what to do.'

CHAPTER FOUR

Before we left the ship at La Ceiba, Emily tried to kiss me. She said she would be my girlfriend, if I wanted. I said all right, but it had to be a secret. She touched my arm and ran away. I didn't get a chance to speak to her again on the ship, and at the docks the three families were soon separated.

We stayed in a small hotel near the beach at La Ceiba. The beach was dirty. Cows walked on it. There were small houses close to the water; the houses weren't suitable for animals, but people were living in them. Near the shore, the sea was thick with plastic bottles and old fruit. The smell was awful. Nearly everyone we saw was wearing a gun. Once, at the edge of the town, we saw a dead dog lying in the street, with **vultures** pulling pieces from its stomach.

I was afraid. We were so far from home. On the beach, Father and Mother walked in front of us, holding hands and whispering. We followed and I thought – What now?

Jerry said, 'I hate it here.'

'Don't let him hear you,' I said.

◆

Father was always busy, as usual, and always talking. He seemed to love it here. He sang as he walked around the town. He brought different people back to the hotel every day, and talked business with them. One of his new friends, a black man called Mr Haddy, was often there. One day, Father brought back an old German he called Karl, and paid him four hundred dollars for a place called Jeronimo. The German described it as a small town. Father told us about it.

'There are no policemen there, no telephones, no electricity, no aeroplanes – nothing. It's about as unimportant as a place can be. We talk about starting from nothing, and Jeronimo is nothing.'

That was the day our ship, the *Unicorn*, left. I felt lonely, lost. Our last contact with home was gone. After that, I never left Father's side. I sat quietly in shops while he bought all kinds of tools, pipes and **tanks** and metal **equipment**. He said he would need them in Jeronimo.

Father had brought us here. Now, in some magical way, he had bought a town. I didn't know why. I only knew that whatever he was doing, he was doing it among the savages.

8

CHAPTER FIVE

Mr Haddy had a boat, the *Little Haddy*. It was a typical Honduras boat – the kind of boat people in America threw out as useless. But this was the boat in which we were going to go to Santa Rosa, the nearest town on the coast to Jeronimo, which was on the Aguan River.

Father found a lot of men to help him put all the equipment into the boat. We had been in La Ceiba less than a week, and already he seemed to be friendly with nearly everyone he met.

I heard him say to Mother, 'It's a funny thing. They're helping me because they think I'm strong. If I was weak, they wouldn't help at all. It should be just the opposite. And you're wondering why these people are savages?'

It was a ten-hour journey to Santa Rosa. We had to travel at night, because the sea was calmer then. The younger children soon fell asleep around Mother. I fell asleep listening to Father arguing with Mr Haddy.

'Let me drive the boat, Mr Haddy.'

'No, it's against the rules.'

'What rules?'

'You're the passenger, I'm the captain – those are the rules.'

'If I was the type of person to be a passenger, I'd still be back up north in the United States, with all those unhappy people.' Then he started to tell Mr Haddy that there was so much crime in the States that it was nearly at war, and soon there would be a full war. The last words I heard were 'America's finished.'

When I woke up, it was still dark. Father was driving the

boat and I couldn't see Mr Haddy anywhere. I asked Father where he was.

'I threw him over the side,' he answered.

I believed everything Father said. I looked over the side. Mother said, 'He's only joking. Mr Haddy's asleep.'

Mr Haddy appeared not long afterwards. 'Father's driving my boat,' he said in surprise. 'Last night he made himself the captain. I told him it was against the rules, but he didn't listen.'

I think we were all secretly glad. Father was controlling another man's boat on a coast he had never seen before. It seemed to show that he could do anything.

'We'll be in Santa Rosa for breakfast,' Mr Haddy said.

'I've got news for you, sir,' Father said. 'We're going to have breakfast here in the boat. Look what Mother and I caught while the rest of you were asleep.' He held up five fat fish. 'You and Mother prepare these fish,' he went on, 'and then you can eat *real* food.'

While they were preparing the fish, Father said, 'I'll tell you another thing. We're not stopping at Santa Rosa. I've been looking at the map.'

'Father and his map,' Mr Haddy complained. 'What's wrong with Santa Rosa?'

'I don't want to meet any missionaries,' Father said. 'And the river's deep enough. You go up to the front and look out for rocks.'

'Be careful,' Mr Haddy cried. 'This is a sea-boat, not a pipanto!'* But he obeyed Father's orders.

We left the ocean behind us. Out on the sea, the boat had seemed small and weak, but here on the river the noise of its engine was loud and birds flew out of the trees on the river

* Pipanto: a Central American river boat.

10

'Look what Mother and I caught while the rest of you were asleep.' He held up five fat fish.

banks. It was our first sight of real jungle. We passed a few other boats – pipantos – going the other way.

'How far are we going?' Mother asked Father, after about fifteen miles.

'Until we hit bottom,' Father said.

On one of the side streams, I saw men in the trees – black, shiny-skinned men. I went up to the front of the boat and asked Mr Haddy about them. He called them Zambus. He took his eyes off the river for a moment to look at them – and the boat hit a rock. Father jumped over the side with a **rope** and tied the boat to a tree. The water came up to his waist. There was a hole in the side of Mr Haddy's boat.

'Mr Haddy,' Father called, 'ask these men where we are!'

But before Mr Haddy could say a thing, seven or eight

men appeared on a muddy path that led to the bank. They were wearing shorts and carrying nets and sticks. Mr Haddy began to speak to them in English.

Father was tying another rope, so that the boat was out of the **current** and close to the bank. 'They speak English?' he cried, and began to laugh.

This pleased the black men. One of them said, 'Good morning, Father. My name is Francis Lungley. Can we help you?'

Father said, 'We've arrived.'

CHAPTER SIX

Jeronimo, just a name, was the muddy end of the muddy path. Because it had once been a **clearing**, the plants grew more thickly here than in the jungle itself. In other ways, it was no different from a dozen other places we had passed. It was hot, smelly and full of insects. The German's broken-down house looked sad and useless. We could see among the jungle plants an old chair in which someone had started a fire.

We looked around helplessly. But Father was shouting, 'Nothing! Nothing! This is what I dreamed about, Mother – nothing!'

Mother said, 'You're right. I don't see a thing.'

'Do you see it, Charlie?'

I said no, but he was pushing his way through the chest-high plants, pointing excitedly here and there.

'I see a house here,' he said. 'Over there, our fields, with vegetables growing. We'll get chickens and keep them here. Over there, a building for me to work in. We'll make that stream run into our fields, and fill our water-tank over there.

'Nothing! Nothing! This is what I dreamed about,
Mother – nothing!'

We'll lift the house up a bit because when it rains here, it rains hard. We can have a pump here and a bath-house there, and – '

All this time the Zambus and Mr Haddy were bringing the equipment from the boat. Father went on talking, marking where the house would be, and where we would put stones for paths. We had arrived ten minutes ago.

But even Father's excited voice could not make Jeronimo more than it was – a smelly old clearing with a broken-down house.

Father came back, saying, 'It's beautiful. That must be Karl's house. You won't find me living there.'

Mr Haddy said, 'There are already people inside.'

Faces appeared at the windows and stared white-eyed at us through climbing flowers. Father went up to the house, picked a flower and said to one of the faces, 'What's your name?'

'Maywit,' came the nervous answer.

'That's the name of the flower,' Mr Haddy whispered to me. 'It's not their name.'

We put our tent under a tree and built a smoky fire to keep the mosquitoes away. Mother hung our food bags on the branches – we had already seen rats.

We sat down to eat. During the meal the Maywits came, carrying plates of fruit. This family too was a father, a mother and four children. 'Everyone,' said Father, 'I want you to meet our neighbours, the Maywits.'

'Is that your real name?' Mr Haddy asked.

'Don't listen to him,' Father said. 'Sit down with us. You can stay in that house. I have some work for you to do. You can stay as long as you work. OK?'

The man said yes. The whole family sat down near the other Zambus. Father started to tell them about the journey from Hatfield, and about how there was going to be a war in America, but it was clear that they didn't understand much of what he was saying, and were just laughing at the long words.

Father said he did not believe in accidents. 'I was looking for you,' he said, 'and you were looking for me. Why were you down by the river?'

Francis Lungley said, 'I don't know why I went to the river. I just had to go. Then I saw the boat.'

'I don't know why I looked out of the window,' Mr Maywit said. 'Then I saw this man from the United States, standing in the grass. That is why I looked out.'

Mr Haddy said, 'I had a dream about a man, and this is the same man. I met him in my dream.'

But I knew Mr Haddy was lying. He had told me himself he had met Father at the La Ceiba docks and thought he was a missionary. But I didn't say anything because I didn't want to break the quiet, serious mood.

'I was sent here,' Father said. 'I'm not going to tell you who sent me, or why. And I'm not going to tell you who I am, or what I plan to do. I'm going to *show* you why I'm here.'

My father hadn't slept for two nights and his voice sounded tired. 'You're going to see food growing here, and fresh water, and hot water, and good buildings, and chickens. You're going to see things you've never seen before.'

No one spoke; they were all listening.

'Now, go to bed,' said Father. 'I'll stay by the fire.' Jerry and the twins and Mother were already asleep in our tent.

'Why don't you sleep?' Mr Haddy asked.

Father said, 'I never sleep.'

CHAPTER SEVEN

Everything that Father had imagined about Jeronimo came true, and more quickly than anyone had thought possible. As we cut down the grass and jungle plants, we kept finding useful tools that Karl had left behind, and even a pile of hard wood. Each time this happened, Father laughed and repeated that there were no accidents. We *had* to be here, we *had* to find these things just when we needed them.

In only a few weeks, the beans we had bought in Springfield were half grown. Jeronimo was starting to look like a real farm and a real home. There were paths, houses, buildings, gardens, a pump.

Father looked around proudly and said, 'You feel a little like God.'

But these first weeks in Jeronimo were not easy. In Hatfield, we had done what we wanted most of the time. Here it was work, and then more work, from the moment we woke up until bedtime. By midday, the heat was terrible. It often rained in the afternoon, but only for a short time, and then Father made us go back to work. As well as all our jobs in the fields or making things, we had to have a shower once a day in the bath-house and wash our clothes every day too. The Maywits copied us. They were the only Indians who stayed. Francis Lungley and the others came to see us from time to time. Mr Haddy had left as soon as his boat was repaired.

Father had covered the front bit of the house with mosquito nets, and in the evenings we all used to sit outside. Sometimes the Maywits joined us. Mr Maywit told us about the Indians who lived in the mountains and up the river. Father listened carefully to this information, but he was impatient if the Maywits started talking about their gods. He seemed to want them to believe that *he* was their god.

Father worked harder than anyone. He was always awake before the rest of us, and went to sleep later than us. And the harder he worked, the happier he was. He hated anyone to get ill. He always seemed to think that they were pretending to be ill. And it was true that he himself never got ill. 'I haven't the time to get sick,' he said.

One day, Mr Haddy returned. By then, Father had started working on a mysterious building at the edge of the clearing. He wouldn't tell us what it was. He heard a boat coming up the river and sent me up a tall tree to look. 'Who is it?' he said, sounding angry for the first time in Jeronimo.

'It's the *Little Haddy*,' I replied.

Father was glad about this, but when he got down to the river, he didn't like what he saw. Mr Haddy was not alone. There was a man with him – a white man, carrying a suitcase.

'I've brought you some real food from Santa Rosa,' Mr Haddy said.

Father was not interested. 'Who's this?' he asked.

'Mr Struss from Santa Rosa. He's a paying passenger.'

'How do you do?' the man said, stepping forward. 'You've made yourself a beautiful home. I've been here before. Mr Roper knows me. Don't you, Mr Roper?'

He was speaking to Mr Maywit.

Father said, 'There's no Mr Roper here. The heat is making you mad.'

Mr Maywit stared and kept his mouth shut.

The man was confused. He said, 'I came here to ask you all a question.'

'We're not interested in your questions,' Father said.

17

'I'm glad I came,' Struss said. 'My question is: do you know Jesus?'

'Go away,' Father said.

'You can't answer for all these people here,' Mr Struss said, smiling.

'I didn't hear you ask a question,' Father said. 'You can't ask questions here. I own this place, and I won't let you even step on to the river bank. If you want to talk to these people, you'll have to leave Jeronimo first.'

'God sent me here,' explained Mr Struss.

'Rubbish,' Father said. 'God doesn't know about Jeronimo. If he did, he'd make it a better place. Instead, *I* have to mend it and make it better.'

'God wants me here,' Mr Struss said.

'But we don't,' said Father.

Mr Struss left on foot; Mr Haddy stayed with us. Later Father asked Mr Maywit if he knew Jesus. He said, 'Yes', but laughed nervously.

He then asked all the rest of us, one by one. We all said 'yes' and laughed along with him.

CHAPTER EIGHT

The days passed. They were thick with heat and dust, and the nights were filled with the noise of insects and the cries of birds.

Nobody knew or could guess what Father was building. It was tall and square. It had no windows and only one entrance – a **hatch** high up, with a ladder up to it. It was a plain wooden building, made out of the hard wood we had found – a box with a metal top. It was filled with tanks and pipes. It didn't look as if it belonged in the jungle.

Nobody knew or could guess what Father was building.

No one could guess; but I knew. One day, Father said to me, 'Tell them, Charlie. What is it?'

I remembered. 'Fat Boy,' I said.

As soon as it was built, lots of people came to see it. They were Indians from the hills, Zambus and Spanish-speaking farmers. Some of them stayed in Jeronimo – Mr Harkins and Mr Peaselee, John Dixon and old Mrs Kennywick. Father put them to work. We needed all the workers we could get.

Father talked about Fat Boy as if it was alive: he said things like, 'I'm working on his heart now.' And the people were afraid of Fat Boy. They said they heard noises inside it at night. No one would go inside unless Father went first. One morning Mr Harkins said that it had gone. We ran out of the house and saw it was there. 'It just came back,' he said.

'This isn't something to be afraid of,' Father said. 'It isn't new; it isn't magic. It isn't even an invention. People call me an inventor, but everything we make is just copied from the natural world. Aeroplanes are big birds; computers are brains. The only bad and useless inventions are unnatural inventions. There are plenty of those in America.'

The Zambus stared at Father and the others listened nervously to this man who always talked as much as he worked.

'What's a savage?' he said. 'A savage is someone who doesn't look around and see that he can change the world.'

Before the floor was finished, he made me and all the adults climb up the pipes inside Fat Boy, all the way to the hatch. He said it would stop us being afraid of it. But when I was inside – in the dark, among the hundreds of pipes – I thought that Fat Boy was a model of my father's mind, and he wanted us to see inside him.

◆

When Fat Boy was finished, Father and Mr Haddy went to

Trujillo, which was the nearest town of any size, to get the **chemicals** Fat Boy needed.

With Father away, Jeronimo was much quieter. We still had work to do, but Mother let us play as well. Together with the Maywit children – Alice, Drainy, Leon and Peewee – we found a path away from the river and into a part of the jungle that was thick with screaming birds. We had brought food with us, and we sat down and ate next to a deep pool.

Day after day, we came back to the same place. We built a **shelter** there out of branches, drank water from the pool, and called the place Home. The Maywit children showed us plants that were good to eat. We tied a rope to a tree and played on it. We pretended to be teachers and students at a school; we pretended to use telephones and listen to the radio.

We still helped at Jeronimo, but when the work was finished we escaped to our Home in the jungle, returning to all the things Father hated. We were as proud of Home as Father was of Jeronimo – and sometimes I thought we had done even better than Father. He had brought seeds with him on the ship, but we ate wild plants. He used nets to keep the mosquitoes away, but we used the juice of leaves.

One day Alice was worried about Drainy playing too near the pool. 'Drainy Roper,' she said, 'you come away from there now.'

Clover said, 'You called him Drainy Roper. That's the name the missionary called you before Father threw him out.'

'That's our name,' Peewee said.

'If your name is Roper, why are you called Maywit?' Jerry asked.

'Your father gave us the name, and my father took it,' Alice said.

'If it wasn't his name,' I said, 'why did he take it?'

'He was afraid.'

'Of Father?'

She nodded.

'I understand,' I said. 'Sometimes I'm afraid of him too.'

CHAPTER NINE

'This is why I'm here,' Father said. 'This is why I came.'

He was standing in front of Fat Boy with a box of matches. There was wood in the fire-box at the bottom of Fat Boy.

'You still don't know what he does, do you?' Father asked.

'It's for cooking,' Mr Haddy said.

'No guesses,' Father said. 'You saw Lungley and Dixon put those bowls of water inside the tanks. Now we're going to light a fire here with this match. You won't believe your eyes.'

He let Peewee start the fire – 'because you're the youngest. You'll still be here when the rest of us have gone, and you can tell your grandchildren about this great day.'

The Zambus put their hands over their ears when the wood was burning. Father laughed. 'It's true that the chemicals inside Fat Boy are dangerous. But if they didn't **explode** when I was putting them in, they won't explode now.'

We waited. Smoke started to come out of the top, and Fat Boy's stomach began to make noises. A few minutes later, Father climbed the ladder and disappeared through the hatch.

'I hope it's safe in there,' Mr Haddy said.

'Quiet,' someone whispered.

Father's head re-appeared in the open hatch. He waved his hand. There was something white in his hand. He threw it down to the ground. It made a noise as it hit the ground and the Indians jumped.

'Haven't you ever seen snow?' Father shouted.

22

♦

Every day now, Indians came out of the jungle to look at Fat Boy. Father gave them ice if they did some work for him. But they didn't come for the ice; they came to stare at Fat Boy, which they thought was some kind of god.

'What is ice good for?' little Leon Maywit asked.

And Father explained that it let us control our lives: we could keep food fresh, live healthier lives. 'Ice is what makes us different from savages,' he said.

But in fact we didn't *need* ice. We were living off fresh food; we weren't unhealthy. It was just something new. It was a way for Father to control things.

Father planned to take ice to some Indians who had never seen it before — who had perhaps never seen a white man before. Francis Lungley told him about a village called Seville, several hours up the river, where the people lived in trees and still had tails. 'That's where we're going,' said Father.

He made a big **block** of ice and we put it into the new pipanto we had built. Clover and I went with him and Mr Haddy. We travelled for hours up the river. The block of ice was covered in banana leaves. We passed several small dirty villages on the river bank, but each time Father told us to continue. He saw signs that white men had been there.

'At Brewer's Lagoon, where I lived when I was a child,' Mr Haddy said, 'there are plenty of villages which are rubbish. We should be there.'

At last we arrived at a village which we recognized as Seville from Francis's description. It was even smaller and dirtier than the rest. We saw a snake swimming in the river. Faces stared at us from the trees, but when we entered the village, it was empty. The houses were made out of mud, instead of the usual branches.

At last we arrived at a village which we recognized as Seville from
Francis's description. It was even smaller and dirtier than the rest.

'This is the place!' Father cried happily. 'They've been savages for two thousand years!'

'I don't like it here,' said Mr Haddy. 'Why don't we go home. We could kill our own mosquitoes,' he added, as a big one landed on his arm.

Father walked around the village with Clover and called into the surrounding jungle. Slowly people began to appear from behind the trees. The women wore torn dresses and the men wore shorts. Most of the children wore nothing at all.

Father said, 'They don't look so bad to me. But this must be the place.'

Father took three of the villagers to our boat. They came back carrying the ice in its covering of banana leaves.

They put the ice on the ground and Father pulled some of the leaves off. He broke off a bit of ice and put it into the headman's hands.

'What do you think about that?' he asked.

'Good morning to you, sir,' the headman replied. 'Monday, Tuesday, Friday. Thank you, that is a good lesson.'

Father turned to us and smiled. 'He doesn't understand a thing.'

Drops of water fell from the man's hands.

Father pointed at the ice and said, 'What's that?'

'Hice,' said the headman.

'Jesus Christ!' shouted my father. He pushed the headman angrily. But as soon as he spoke, all the villagers fell to their knees and started saying, 'Our Father in heaven . . .'

Mr Haddy was laughing softly. Father shouted at them, turned and went back to the boat. We stayed and talked to the villagers. They had seen ice four or five times before: missionaries had brought it. They called it cold stones that turned to water. They believed that we were missionaries too, and that Father was our leader.

On the way back down the river, Father was silent and in a bad mood. That night in Jeronimo, I heard Mother talking to him as if he was a child, telling him he was brilliant and that she was proud of him.

CHAPTER TEN

One evening in November, Father stood in the centre of Jeronimo and pointed with his half-finger at the mountains in the distance.

'That's next,' he said. 'We'll take them an even bigger block of ice.'

And a few days later, he woke Jerry and me up before the sun was up. 'We're all ready,' he said. 'I've been up for hours.'

'Father doesn't need any sleep,' Mr Haddy said.

When my eyes became used to the darkness, I could see Mr Maywit looking after an enormous block of ice. The ice was tied to a **sled**, which Father had made to pull the ice through the jungle.

'Where are my jungle men?' Father said, and Francis Lungley, John Dixon and Mr Peaselee stepped out of the darkness. Mr Maywit was staying in Jeronimo.

Father went in front, then came the Zambus pulling the sled, and Jerry and I were last.

Father talked as he walked, about America and its troubles. Very soon we were walking uphill, and it was hard for Jerry and me to keep up with the men. But we were on a path, and whenever the Zambus had to pull the sled round a corner, they slowed down and then Jerry and I caught up with them.

By the time we had climbed for half an hour, there was

Very soon we were walking uphill, and it was hard for Jerry and me to keep up with the men.

enough light to look back and see Jeronimo below us. We could see people busy at their work – Mrs Kennywick feeding the chickens, Mr Haddy going to the bath-house.

'Mother,' Francis said, and pointed. She was hanging clothes on the washing-line.

'She's all business,' Father said proudly.

But she wasn't. She was calmer, and always asked us if we were hungry or tired, or if there was anything we wanted. She let us leave Jeronimo and find Home. Father seemed to imagine that we were adults, but we were children – sometimes wishing we were back in America, afraid of the dark and not very strong. Mother knew that. Father was strong and he couldn't understand that other people might not be.

'Another mile,' Father was saying, 'and then we'll be at the top. After that, it's all downhill.'

But when we thought we had reached the top, we saw the mountain stretching further up in front of us.

Jerry said, 'I want to rest. Will you wait for me, Charlie?'

'Dad won't like it. We can't sit down while they're doing all the work.' But I felt sorry for Jerry, and I ran up to Father to ask if we could rest.

'He's only pretending to be tired,' Father replied, and continued walking. 'When we get to the top, we'll stop for lunch, and then we'll just run this sled of ice down to those wild men.'

But the mountain just went on and on. Up here the trees were thinner and burnt by the sun. It was very hot, and I could hear the Zambus breathing hard. Soon, there was so much water coming from under the banana leaves covering the ice that Jerry and I were walking in mud.

Finally, we had to stop for lunch, although we were still not at the top. The Zambus were too tired to speak. But we didn't rest for long, because Father saw how much ice had gone. 'Why didn't you say something, Charlie? Come on, let's hurry!'

But by the middle of the afternoon, we still hadn't reached the top of the mountain. The Zambus wanted to make Father happy so much that they hurried – and ran the sled into a rock. Both the sled and the block of ice broke down the middle.

'That's wonderful,' Father said quietly. 'That is just what I need. Thank you very much. I'm just going for a little walk. You stay here, and if you want to pick up the pieces, I promise I won't stop you.' He gave us all a weak smile.

He disappeared. A minute later we heard him scream from the jungle.

'He's very angry,' I said to the Zambus. 'You'd better fix this.'

The Zambus cut the ice free and, complaining, made two

sleds. It was almost an hour before we could start again, and now the ice was even smaller.

The sun was losing its heat, and the mosquitoes came out. Jerry and I used the leaf juice to keep them away, but Father said, 'If you're frightened of a few insects, you shouldn't be here!' He was soon covered in mosquito bites.

I said, 'We'll have to go home in the dark.'

'We can't go home until we deliver this ice.'

Deliver it where? I looked at the ice. There was not much left.

When night came, Father said. 'All right. Let's stop and sleep.'

'Where?' Jerry asked.

'Just there, across the street, in the hotel, of course. Where did you think? I hope they've got comfortable beds.'

Jerry started to cry.

It was clear that Father had not planned to stay out for the night. We had eaten most of the food. We had no tents or mosquito nets, no lamps or blankets. The water-bag was almost empty.

I started to make a shelter with some branches, like the one in Home, and Father said, 'Suddenly Charlie knows all about how to live in the jungle.'

I offered him some plants to eat, but he said he wasn't hungry. 'I don't eat rats and grass.'

Later, as I was trying to sleep, I opened my eyes and saw him sitting in front of the block of ice. I could see his shape against the night sky.

'I want to sleep in my own bed!' he screamed. He couldn't control his life here.

I tried to think of something to say.

'What are you looking at?' he asked. 'This is the first time ever that water from ice has touched the ground here. Think of it! And you're saying that's nothing?'

CHAPTER ELEVEN

The journey was easier the next day. There were only two pieces of ice to carry, each the size of a football. And we soon reached the top of the mountain. The view was wonderful: all Honduras was there in front of us. We could probably see all the way to Nicaragua. We started downhill.

We almost didn't see the village; the smell of smoke told us we were close, and then we saw women on their knees in the mud by a stream.

'Those women are washing clothes,' I said.

Jerry said, 'So what?'

'No one's wearing clothes,' I said. 'Not that kind.'

The women ran away when we came near, and the men in the village stared at us.

'They've probably never seen a white man before,' whispered Father. 'No one must make a sudden noise or movement.' We stayed behind him.

He tried talking to the men in English and then in Spanish, but they didn't seem to understand. He offered them the bag in which he had put one of the pieces of ice. One of the men opened the bag and turned it upside down. Only water ran out on to the ground.

'Quick!' Father said. 'The other bag.'

The Indians watched Father searching in the wet bag. 'Got it!' Father said, and held up a small piece of ice, the size of my little finger. He put it in his open hand to show them, and the little piece of ice immediately disappeared. Before they could look at it, the water ran between his fingers.

Father still held his wet hand out, but the Indians were staring at his half-finger.

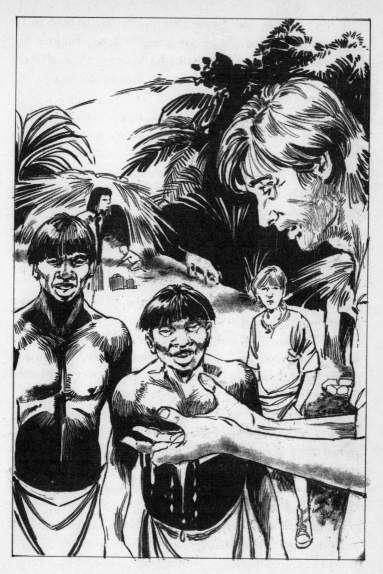

*He put it in his open hand to show them, and the little piece
of ice immediately disappeared.*

'I don't believe this,' Father said quietly. He walked away. For a moment, I thought he was going back to Jeronimo, but he turned and began to talk to the Indians. He told them about the ice he had brought them. 'I'll be back!' he said. 'I'll show you.'

But most of the Indians were still staring at his half-finger.

Then one of them spoke, very clearly, in Spanish. 'Go away!' he said.

Father laughed at him.

'I'm sorry,' he said. 'It was an accident. Next time, I'll get the ice to you.'

'Go away,' the Indian said again. But he looked frightened, not frightening.

'These are real savages,' Father said.

'We should go,' Francis said.

'I'm not moving,' Father said. 'Charlie, tell them we're not going until we've eaten something.'

I told them. The Indians went away, and we sat down under a tree. Although I was tired and hungry, I wanted to get out of this place, and I knew from Jerry's face that he did too.

To our complete surprise, the food was brought to us by white men! They looked ill, but they were almost smiling, and as they put the food in front of us, they watched us closely.

'This is what the Indians didn't want us to see,' Father said. 'These men are their prisoners!'

He spoke to the men in Spanish. 'Hey! Do you let these Indians tell you what to do?'

'Yes.'

The Indians watched us from the other side of the clearing.

'Where are you from?' asked one of the men. 'Are you missionaries?'

'Do I look like a missionary?' Father asked. 'No, we live across the mountains. We have a small farm there. If you can escape, you'd be safe. That's the best way to the coast.'

The man nodded. 'Why did you come here?'

Father explained about the ice, and how he made it.

'Your father is an intelligent man,' the man said to me.

'Everyone says that,' I said.

Father said, 'They'll keep you here until you're too weak to work, and then they'll kill you and feed you to the vultures. Do you think they'll try to get us?'

'Who knows? They're very strong,' the man said, and the other men nodded.

'I want to walk out of here wearing my head,' Father said. 'I want to get back home. We have everything there.'

'Guns?' the man asked.

'No, no guns. We don't need them. You know, you remind me of how I used to feel in the United States, like a prisoner. I just got up and walked away. If you take my advice, you'll do the same.'

'We might do that,' the man said. 'How far is it to your farm?'

Father told them. 'You'll be safe there,' he said.

The men nodded and smiled. 'But now go,' their leader said. 'You'll help us if you don't make the Indians angry.'

We just got up and left them like that – the Indians sitting on the ground, the white men standing. I was wondering why the prisoners asked so many questions.

◆

The journey back was easier. Father said, 'I wish Mother had seen the Indians' faces when we gave them the ice.'

Jerry was searching Father's face.

'They couldn't believe it!' Father said.

33

Finally, because no one was saying anything, I said, 'What ice?'

'The ice I showed them.'

'There was no ice, Dad.'

'That small piece,' he said. 'You saw it, didn't you, Jerry?'

'Yes, Dad.'

This wasn't true. Father's lie made me feel lonelier than any lie I had ever heard.

◆

Back in Jeronimo, things had changed. The place felt empty. Mother came out of the house; her face was white. 'Allie,' she said, and stopped.

'What has happened?' Father asked.

She said, 'I thought something had happened to you too.'

'Too?'

'The Maywits have gone, all of them. I couldn't stop them.'

Clover and April came running out from the trees. Clover said, 'A motor boat came and took all the Maywits away. It was that missionary.'

'I'll tell you something,' Father said. 'Those Maywits have got a lot to learn.'

If he knew everything, why didn't he know their real name? I said, 'Maywit isn't their name. It's Roper. They're all Ropers.'

'Who says?'

I told him what Alice had told us, but I didn't tell him about Home or that they were all afraid of him. Jerry, Clover and April said nothing; they let me take the blame for knowing.

'Is there more you ought to tell me?' Dad asked.

Mother came out of the house; her face was white.

I was going to say – Those men you called prisoners didn't look like prisoners, and the Indians looked frightened. The ice was gone before they could see it. You wouldn't let us rest, you made Jerry cry.

But I said, 'No.'

'Then I know more than you. I know they'll come back.'

'It was horrible,' Mother said, and Mr Haddy nodded. 'That missionary shouted angrily at the Maywits . . . Ropers. He called you a bad man. He said a lot of the Indians thought you had made a god in a box – Indians he thought were Christians. He pushed the Maywits into the river, to clean them, he said.'

'He said you were as bad as the soldiers,' Clover added.

'What soldiers?'

Mr Haddy said, 'There are soldiers up in the jungle near Nicaragua.'

'The Maywits were frightened,' Mother said. 'They packed their bags and left.'

'They'll be back,' Father said. 'They'll find it's a terrible world out there, and they'll come back. You remember my words.'

◆

Father's next plan was to dig a hole until he reached water. It was the dry season, and the river was low. To save water, we weren't making any ice. Everyone who came for ice was put to work digging the hole. Soon, the visitors stopped coming.

We were fetching water from the river early one morning when Mr Haddy came running out of the jungle towards Father's hole. He stopped at the edge and said to Father, 'People are coming.'

Father climbed out of the hole and said, 'It must be the Maywits. I told you.'

But this time Father was wrong.

'Men,' Mother said, looking up the path. 'Three of them, Allie.'

'I knew they would come too,' Father said, but his voice had gone cold. 'They're the prisoners I told you about.'

'Then why do they have guns, Dad?' Clover asked.

CHAPTER TWELVE

At that moment, I knew how the people in Seville felt, and how all the others felt, when we came out of the jungle. We stepped into their villages like this, big and strange and uninvited.

What did these men want? Their clothes were the ones I had seen the Indians washing.

'Hello,' Father said to them. 'How are you?'

The men were silent, and kept their hands on their guns. They looked carefully around Jeronimo before replying. Their leader said, 'We didn't think we would find you.'

'Here we are,' Father said.

'How many people are there here?' asked the man.

'Just us,' my father said.

'I don't like these men,' Mr Haddy whispered to me. The Zambus had disappeared into the jungle.

'You're just in time for breakfast,' Father said.

'Where are the Zambus you brought with you across the mountains?' the man asked.

'They saw your guns and hid in the jungle,' Father said. 'They're probably putting poison on their knives now.'

The men looked worried.

'Don't worry,' Father said. 'We'll keep you safe. But we have only enough food for ourselves. We can't feed you as well. After breakfast, you'd better go down river to the coast. It isn't far.'

'We'll think about your suggestion.'

In the middle of the morning, the three men went into the jungle with their guns. They didn't return until the evening. We thought they had gone.

'Have your Zambus come back?' they asked.

'No, there's no sign of them,' Father said. He seemed less worried now, as if he'd solved a problem.

During the evening meal, the men asked Father how he had lost half his finger.

Father laughed and said, 'Yes, that's an interesting story. It was our first night here in Jeronimo. We were all sleeping in tents, under mosquito nets. I dreamt that I was pushing on a doorbell. I pushed my finger through the mosquito net and one of those enormous jungle rats bit it off! You're not in the mountains any more, you know: this is real jungle here. I'm glad I didn't push my whole hand through the net. There are all sorts of snakes and insects and wild animals here. If anyone slept outside here, there'd be nothing left of him in the morning.'

The men looked at one another. They had hot, nervous eyes.

'Where are you sleeping tonight?' Father asked.

'We like it here,' the leader said.

'You had better go far away from here,' Father said. And for the rest of the evening, whenever one of the men was staring at him, Father lifted his half-finger.

But the men showed no signs of leaving. They sat there with their guns across their knees. Either they did nothing, or they played with April and Clover.

Father's mood changed; he became quieter. He went over to Fat Boy, climbed the ladder and did some work on the hatch. When he came back down and saw the men again, he began laughing. It was dark now. Mr Haddy brought a lamp. I stood watching with Jerry.

Father was still laughing. He said, 'I'm a fool. You said you liked it here, and I didn't believe you. But you meant what you said, didn't you? You're staying the night here, aren't you?'

'Yes. We'll stay until we're ready to go.'

'I'm not a savage,' Father said. 'I'm not going to make you prisoners. But it's dark now. You can't go anywhere. You are our guests now, and I must give you somewhere safe to sleep – away from insects and animals and Zambus. Come with me.'

He led them over to Fat Boy. They climbed up the ladder and went in through the hatch.

◆

Father woke me after midnight. The air was full of the noise of insects. He put his hand over my mouth so that I wouldn't make a noise.

'Get your shoes and follow me,' he whispered.

I followed him across the clearing towards Fat Boy. He was carrying a thick piece of wood under his arm.

'I gave them a chance to leave,' he said, 'but they refused. You heard them. They're planning to stay here and feed off us like mosquitoes feed off our blood. I was wrong about them being prisoners of the Indians.'

'The Indians looked frightened,' I said.

'Did they? When I make a mistake, I certainly make a big one.' He was staring up at Fat Boy. He said, almost to himself, 'We kill mosquitoes without pity.'

I didn't know what to say.

'Charlie,' he said, 'I've fixed the hatch so that you can lock it completely with this piece of wood. Can you climb up the ladder and do it, without making a sound?'

'I think so,' I said.

'You'd better be sure,' Father said, 'because if you make any noise, those insects are going to start shooting.'

I did what he wanted. Those three minutes were the longest minutes of my life.

When I got back down to the ground, Father said, 'Look! Someone has left the fire burning under Fat Boy.'

But there was no fire. He put a match to the pile of small sticks and bits of wood. 'Somebody started a fire here,' he said, 'and I told them not to.' His face was wild. 'We'll just have to let it burn. There's nothing we can do to stop it.'

'The men –' But what could I tell him that he did not already know? He knew the men inside would freeze to death.

'Start counting, Charlie. By the time you get to three hundred, there won't be any men in there.'

He said no more. He led me back towards the house. Before we got there, we heard noises from inside Fat Boy. The men were hitting their guns against the sides. Then they started shooting.

'Allie, are you all right?' It was Mother.

The shooting continued. There was the sound of bullets hitting the metal pipes as well as the wooden sides.

'Keep counting, Charlie.'

Clover, April and Jerry appeared next to Mother. April was crying. We could just hear the men screaming. Mr Haddy came and asked what was happening.

'They're damaging him,' Father said. He was not frightened, but hurt and angry. 'They won't lie down. They're going to make a hole in him.'

He spoke as if something in his own head was breaking.

Then the explosion came. It filled the clearing with light that made every leaf turn red and gold. All the buildings shook. It lifted Fat Boy from the ground, broke it and dropped it back down again. Burning gas shot into the air.

I could see Father shouting something, but the noise was so great that none of us could hear him. When we did, he was saying, 'Follow me! Follow me! We'll all be poisoned!'

The fire was spreading fast. The nearest buildings were already burning, and so were all the trees around Fat Boy. Father said, 'Cover your faces and follow me.' But he couldn't move.

I said, 'I know a place –'

As I started walking, the others followed. I found that I was still counting. I led them towards Home. Behind us, more explosions shook the night.

Behind us, more explosions shook the night.

CHAPTER THIRTEEN

All that night, Fat Boy's fire showed over the treetops like a bright hat. Everyone was asleep. I sat through the long night and watched, and thought.

Father, who usually never slept for more than a few hours, and who hated people who stayed in bed late, slept like a dead man, without moving, for thirteen hours. This was almost more frightening than all the rest of the things which had happened. We sat and waited for him to wake up.

When he was awake, we went back to Jeronimo. There was nothing standing; the fire had burnt every building, every plant, every tree. The air smelled strongly of chemicals. The river was full of dead fish.

'It's finished,' Father said.

'All your work,' Mother said. 'I'm so sorry, Allie.'

'I'm happy,' Father said. 'We're free.'

'No,' said Mother. 'All your inventions, all your wonderful machines, all our plants – they've gone.'

'They were like a prison,' Father said. 'I've learnt my lesson. I had to poison a whole river, but I learnt my lesson. Now we can go away.'

'Where?' Mother asked.

'You could come to Brewer's Lagoon,' Mr Haddy said. 'I think I'll go there now.'

'Yes, I like the name,' Father said. 'Let's go.'

'Wait,' Mother said. 'What about your tools? We can find some useful things here still.'

'No,' Father said. 'It's all poisoned. We must leave it all behind. We can make a fresh start. I'm *right*, Mother! America's dead now. The wars have burnt it up. But we're alive.'

Brewer's Lagoon was a large sea-water lake, cut off from the sea by a wide beach. It was muddy and smelly. Father refused to let us live near Mr Haddy's village. We left Mr Haddy there and took the pipanto up the smallest stream until we could go no further. We had reached a smaller, muddier, smellier lake, but at least it wasn't sea water.

'This is it,' Father said. 'This is where we belong.'

There we lived like savages. At first, we had nothing, but every day Father and I went to the coast and brought back bits of rope and wood, torn fishing nets, and all kinds of things. After storms, we sometimes found useful tools. Soon we had a big pile of rubbish behind us, on the bank at the top of the beach. There were several old, broken boats lying on the beach, and Father made one of them into a home for us. He was very pleased with his work, and kept saying that no water could get into our house.

Father said that we were like the first people in the world, specially now that there was no more North America. We would start with nothing – no machines. 'Trees, water and the ground – that's all we need,' he said.

We planted seeds, but it was still the hot season, and we spent all our time carrying water from the lake to try to keep the small plants alive. Father had built a pump, but it needed seven men to make it work. 'Don't worry,' Father said. 'The rains will start soon and then we'll be fine.'

Everyone except Father and me became ill. All we ever did was work, and we ate only sea-birds and small fish. Father was cruel to Jerry while he was ill. He thought he was old enough now not to get ill, to be a real man and work all the time, with little food and sleep.

We saw almost no one. If Mr Haddy came, bringing us

seeds or extra food, Father was rude to him. Once a Zambu passed by, dressed in a clean shirt, on his way to church. Our hair was long, we were thin and dirty and untidy – compared to this Zambu, *we* were the savages.

Day after day, we waited for the rain, but it didn't come. The water in the lake got lower and lower, and one day we found the engine of a boat stuck in the mud. Father now spent all his time cleaning the engine, but there was no petrol in it.

'You're wasting your time with that old engine,' Mother said one day. Her voice travelled over the water to where we were fishing.

'It'll be useful one day,' Father replied.

'You're just a scavenger. You're no different from those sea-birds you hate so much.'

'This scavenger saved your life, Mother. Without me, you'd all be dead.'

'Without you, we'd still be safe in America.'

'America's finished, gone. The world went crazy, and we came here. Do you know a better place?'

'Allie, you'll kill us here!'

Clover said, 'Mother's making trouble again. She's wrong.'

'No,' Jerry said. 'She's right. I want to go away with Mr Haddy the next time he visits.'

April said, 'I want to run away from this awful place.'

We watched Mother leave the boat-house and walk away. She came back in the evening and Jerry asked, 'Mother, how long are we going to stay in this place?'

She did not speak. She stared at Father.

Father said, 'Answer him, Mother.'

'The rest of our lives,' she said.

Jerry asked, 'Mother, how long are we going to stay in this place?'

CHAPTER FOURTEEN

When the rain came, it was like an unbroken wall of water. The noise on the roof of our boat-house was terrible. All our plants were flattened, before they had had a chance to grow. And every day the water of the lake came closer to our home.

One afternoon, when it wasn't raining, Mr Haddy came. Father was away on the coast, scavenging. Mr Haddy brought a big tank of petrol.

'Don't tell him I brought it,' Mr Haddy said. 'Say you found it. The water's coming up, and you must be able to escape.'

I hid the tank of petrol among the rubbish behind our boat-house. Just then Father returned.

'I brought some food,' Mr Haddy said.

'Do you think we can't look after ourselves?' Father said angrily.

'The water's going to come up to your house,' Mr Haddy went on. 'You should come with me to Brewer's Village.'

Father turned to Mother. 'This savage is suggesting . . .'

'Don't be so rude, Allie,' Mother said.

'Who sent you here, Haddy?' Father said. 'Go back and tell him that this is our home now.'

Jerry said, 'I want to go with Mr Haddy.'

'All right, Jerry,' Father said. 'Drop your bucket and go. Just go. But remember: if you go, you can never come back. Not once.'

'Allie!' Mother said.

'That's the rule.'

Jerry began to cry.

46

'Before you go, Haddy,' Father said. 'Look around and tell me what you see.'

'Do you mean all that rubbish?' Mr Haddy said.

'I see a village here,' Father said. 'I see healthy children running around, chickens, plants, big soft beds. I see everyone working all the time. That's the right way to live! And if you don't see it, you don't belong here.'

♦

'Dad's crazy,' Jerry said to me later. 'Didn't you want to go with Mr Haddy too?'

'No,' I said. 'If we don't stay and help him, we'll all die.'

'I don't want to help him. I want to go home.'

'This is home,' I said. 'There's no more America. Didn't you hear what Father said?'

'I don't believe him.'

I asked Mother what had happened to the United States. Was it all burnt and gone, as Father said?

She looked sad and said, 'I hope so.' She pushed my hair out of my eyes and kissed me. 'Because if it is, we're the luckiest people in the world.'

'And if it isn't?'

'Then we're making a horrible mistake.'

♦

Within a week, our garden had gone. The water of the lake washed the last plants away. There was a strong current in the lake now. Our boat-house was starting to shake and move as the water reached it, but all Father could say was how proud he was that no water was getting inside. He had built it well. 'I was right again,' he said. 'I couldn't die if I tried!'

Then one day the water lifted us up, and our boat-house became a true boat.

'The current will take us to the coast,' Jerry said, 'and then I'm going to find Mr Haddy. He'll take us to La Ceiba, and then we can go back to the United States.'

'There's nothing on the coast for us,' Father said. 'It's too easy to let the current take us to the coast – anyone can do that. But we've got an engine.'

'But it doesn't work, Allie,' Mother said.

'But look what I found,' Father said. He pulled a cover off a tank of petrol. 'Some fool had left it in the mud.'

I didn't say anything. We fixed the engine on to the back of the boat, tied the pipanto on and started up the Patuca River.

CHAPTER FIFTEEN

'Allie, we should go to the coast,' Mother said. 'We know what's there.'

'Yes, there are scavengers there,' Father replied. 'There's death there. How can I be wrong if I'm going against the current? When the petrol finishes, we'll pull the boat along. No electricity, no machines, no chemicals. Just hard work. The rest of the world is under water, and this is the future. We are the future.'

Jerry and I had to lie at the front of the boat, looking out for rocks. With Father, Jerry was silent now, but to me he whispered his hate and his fear. April and Clover helped Mother inside.

Every village we passed was under water. At last we found one with some people in. We stopped to get more petrol. Father gave them some tools and a mirror for the petrol. The village was horribly dirty, and the people were thin and

Father gave them some tools and a mirror for the petrol.

hungry. But Father was delighted with them. He congratu-
lated them on their way of life: 'Out there' – he pointed with
his half-finger – 'they're all dead or dying. But you've got it
right!'

Father asked them if there were any villages up river.

'Wumpoo.'

'How far away is that?'

'Two days.'

'Then I'm going a month or a year. I'm going until there's
no more river.'

On the boat, Father said, 'Did they say Wumpoo? I think
I've heard the name before.'

No one remembered. But I remembered. Wumpoo –
Guampu!

◆

Three days later, in the late afternoon, from around a bend in the river, we heard singing. It was church music.

'Who's singing?' April asked.

'Birds,' Father said. 'Or savages.'

'But this might be Guampu,' I said.

We came round the bend and saw small houses with metal roofs. In the middle of a large clearing was a white wooden church. It was all clean, and it looked wonderful.

Clover said, 'Where are we, Dad?'

Father's face was black with anger. His mouth was shut tight, but there was fire in his eyes. He brought the boat over to the side of the river.

'They have real houses,' April said.

'We'll see about that,' Father said.

'Allie, no!' Mother said. 'Let's just go on. We don't know the people here.'

'The Spellgoods live here,' I said. 'Emily told me – the girl on the *Unicorn*.'

'I knew savages lived here,' Father said.

'Allie, maybe they can help us!'

'We don't need help.'

'We're dirty. Look at us!'

'They're hiding here,' Father said, as he jumped off the boat and on to the bank. 'There's no more world left, and they're poisoning this place. I'll teach them a lesson.'

We followed him. The music was coming from inside the church, but when we got there, we found some Indians sitting in front of a television, watching church on TV.

There was no sign of the Spellgoods.

'Back to the boat!' Father said.

'Can't we look around?' Clover asked.

'No. This place isn't real,' Father said.

He drove the boat to the opposite bank of the river, to

50

keep us away from the village, and ordered us to stay inside. We could hear him and Mother talking, but we couldn't hear what they said.

After dark, when everyone was asleep. Jerry and I went outside and found that Father had gone. He had taken the pipanto with him.

'Let's go,' Jerry said, and we swam over to the other side.

The Spellgoods were back, and I knocked on a window of their house until Emily came and opened it. At first she didn't recognize me under my long hair. 'You're dirty,' she said. 'And you've got thinner. Who's that?'

'That's Jerry, my brother. Listen, can we go somewhere safe to talk?'

We went round to the back of the house. Emily started to tell us that she'd just come back from the United States.

'You mean it's still there?' I asked.

'Of course, stupid. What did you think?'

'My father says it's gone up in flames.'

'You're father is even more strange than mine, then,' Emily said.

'Yeah!' said Jerry. 'I knew it. He's been lying to us all the time. I'm going home. I'm not going up river in that boat!'

I said, 'Emily, we're in bad trouble. We must get to the coast. Can you help us?'

But at that moment, all the lights went off. The whole village was in darkness. Jerry and I looked at each other. We knew.

'Goodbye, Emily. We've got to go,' I said.

We ran back to the bank and dived into the water. Mother was waiting for us.

'What's happening?' she asked. 'Where's Father?'

As if to answer her question, an explosion shook the air and flames jumped out of the church windows.

51

'Oh God!' Mother said. 'He's got the petrol.'

The twins woke up and started calling from inside.

'Jerry,' I said, 'get the twins. Mother, come on! We're getting out of here!'

'*Stay where you are!*' It was Father's voice. He was bringing the pipanto next to the boat.

Jerry whispered to me. 'When he climbs up the side, let's hit him on the head with a heavy piece of wood.'

'No, I can't. You do it.'

But as Father pulled himself up on to the boat, we heard the sound of a shot from the other bank of the river. Father fell heavily back into the pipanto.

'Allie!' Mother screamed, and jumped into the pipanto as well. The twins followed.

'Go, Jerry!' I said urgently.

While Jerry was climbing down to the pipanto, I untied it from the boat and then jumped in myself. I heard Father say, 'Don't leave me. I'm hurt Mother. I can't move.'

The current began to take us back down river, towards the coast.

CHAPTER SIXTEEN

When morning came, we could see that the bullet had hit Father in the neck. The man who was never ill couldn't move his body or his legs. He just lay there with his eyes half open. Only his head was alive.

We let the current take us all the way to the coast. It was so fast that it only took a day. All that day, when Father was awake, his talk made no sense; when he was asleep, he screamed in his dreams. 'The scavengers! The vultures! They're the ones who are going to win! The rest of the world

As Father pulled himself up on to the boat, we heard the sound of a shot from the other bank of the river.

is finished. Only the vultures are left!' But often he was silent, with his head on Mother's legs.

On the coast, we lay under some trees, waiting. Mother walked miles every day to the nearest villages, asking for food and medicine, asking for Mr Haddy. The villagers thought she was a crazy woman.

When I slept, I had dreams about food. I dreamed about chocolate cake and cold milk. I dreamed of our kitchen in Hatfield, of going down there at night. I remembered how the kitchen was dark, but the inside of the refrigerator was bright and filled with clean food.

I was having this dream one day when I was woken by Jerry's shouts.

'It's a boat, Dad!'

Father lifted himself up and watched Jerry running towards the edge of the water.

I said, 'It might be Mr Haddy.'

'Where's Mother?'

'She's in the village.'

The twins were asleep next to him, holding hands.

'Go and see who it is,' Father said. 'There's no need to hurry. I'll be here.'

I left him with the twins and ran down the beach. Jerry had already reached the boat. It was not Mr Haddy, but we stood and talked to the man about fishing. He knew Mr Haddy, and we asked the man to tell him we were here. Suddenly we heard a child's thin scream: 'Mother! Mother! Mother!'

'The twins!' Jerry said.

They were awake when we got back to the trees, but there was no sign of Father. But we could see marks, where he had pulled himself across the beach.

A shout came from the other side of the trees: 'Mother!'

He had pulled himself quite a long way. He lay on the other side of a small hill. He was still now. Five birds — vultures — stood over him and held bits of his body in their mouths. I screamed and ran at them, but even as I came near, one of them dug into my father's head and pulled out his tongue.

Mr Haddy paid for our journey home from La Ceiba. Many years have passed since then. A part of me died with Father, but I still fear him. I sometimes seem to hear him crying, 'They're all after me! I am the last man in the world!'

EXERCISES

Vocabulary Work

Look again at the 'Dictionary Words' in this book. Check that you understand all of them.

1 Copy this puzzle and choose 'Dictionary Words' to complete it.

a A wild place, full of trees.   J _ _ _ _ _ _

b A very simple house.   _ _ E _ _ _ _ _

c These birds feed on dead bodies.   _ _ _ _ _ _ R _ _ _

d Someone who tells people about God.   _ _ _ _ _ _ _ O _ _ _ _ _ _

e A large container for water, petrol, etc.   _ _ N _

f The tools you need for a job.   _ _ _ _ I _ _ _ _ _ _

g A machine for moving water, petrol, etc.   _ _ M _

h Very strong thick string.   _ O _ _ _

2 Answer the questions in a few words.

a Which of these can be a **block**? *salt milk jam butter*

b What do **scavengers** live on?

c What would you use a **net** for in the jungle?

d Are you a **savage**? Why not?

e When something **explodes**, what noise does it make?

3 Find the right word for each definition.

a A stream of water, air, electricity, etc.

b A very small door.

c Allie Fox used this to carry the block of ice.

d A new machine which makes life easier.

e A place in the jungle where the trees have been cut down.

Comprehension

Chapters 1–4

1 What did Father think of modern America?

2 Why is Charlie embarrassed by Emily?

Chapters 5–6
3 Why didn't Father want to go to Santa Rosa?
4 What does he plan to do in Jeronimo?

Chapters 7–9
5 Why was Father so rude to Mr Struss?
6 Where did the children go to play?

Chapters 10–11
7 Why was the journey to the mountain village so difficult?
8 Why did the missionary take the Maywits away?

Chapters 12–14
9 What does Father ask Charlie to do to Fat Boy?
10 What did Mother and the children *really* want to do?

Chapters 15–16
11 What does Father tell his family has happened to America?
12 What happens to Father at the end?

Discussion

1 Think of three modern inventions which have changed our lives. Talk about the *good* effects of each, and the *bad* ones.
2 Charlie is 13, and his father embarrasses him. Talk about the ways your family embarrass you by the things they do.
3 Do you think Allie Fox was mad all the time, or only became mad in Honduras? Why do you think so? Give examples.

Writing

1 Either invent a machine which will clean *everything* in your home, or invent one which will do your homework for you. Draw a picture of it and describe how it works in about 100 words.
2 Use your library to find out who invented:
   a the steam engine.

b the helicopter.

c the computer.

Write two or three sentences about each person.

3 You are Charlie. Write a secret letter to Emily Spellgood about your life in Jeronimo. Tell her about your true thoughts and feelings and describe the place called 'Home' to her.

Review

1 This book was once described as 'an enormously exciting adventure story.' Do you agree or not? Why?

2 Describe how Charlie's feelings towards his father change during the book.